The Banshee

by Eve Bunting

Illustrated by Emily Arnold McCully

Clarion Books
Houghton Mifflin Harcourt
Boston   New York
2009

For my father, who saw one
—E.B.

For Ruth, Liam, and Catherine, with love and thanks
—E.A.M.

Clarion Books • 215 Park Avenue South, New York, NY 10003 • Text copyright © 2009 by Edward D. Bunting and Anne E. Bunting Family Trust • Illustrations copyright © 2009 by Emily Arnold McCully • The illustrations were executed in watercolor. • The text was set in 18-point Regula. • All rights reserved. • For information about permission to reproduce selections from this book, write to Permissions, Houghton Mifflin Harcourt Publishing Company, 215 Park Avenue South, New York, NY 10003. • Clarion Books is an imprint of Houghton Mifflin Harcourt Publishing Company. • www.clarionbooks.com • Printed in China • *Library of Congress Cataloging-in-Publication Data* • Bunting, Eve, 1928– • The Banshee / by Eve Bunting ; illustrated by Emily Arnold McCully. • p. cm. • Summary: When Terry wakes up in the middle of the night to horrible screeching, he thinks the Banshee has come to pay his family a visit. • ISBN 978-0-618-82162-4 • [1. Banshees—Fiction. 2. Superstition—Fiction. 3. Family life—Ireland—Fiction. 4. Ireland—Fiction.] I. McCully, Emily Arnold, ill. II. Title. • PZ7.B91527Ban 2009 • [E]—dc22 • 2008014581 • CAL 10 9 8 7 6 5 4 3 2 1

BANSHEE: The ghost figure of a woman who wails or "keens" outside a house where there may be a death; an Irish superstition.

I'm half asleep when I hear her wailing.
"*SCREE . . . SCREE . . .*"
At first I think it's a dream, and then I know it isn't.
I know what it is. The Banshee! Outside our house.

I sit straight up in bed.
Moonlight whitens the room. Gusts of wind rattle the window.
In the bed across from me my brother, Liam, sleeps.

"Liam?" I whisper, but he just mutters "What?" and turns over to face the wall.

"*SCREE . . . SCREE . . .*" There it is again, rising and falling like the waves of the sea.

I put my hands over my ears and slide out of bed.

It's December in Ireland. Cold. The linoleum is ice under my feet.

My parents' room is at the front of the house, down the hall.

I stumble my way along and push open their door. The moon doesn't reach this far, and their room is dark.

My da's snores don't change when I bumble in, but my mother
is awake at once. She slips out of bed.

"Terry? What is it?" she asks. "What's wrong? Is it Liam?"

Liam gets sick sometimes, and my mother is anxious about him. "He's a delicate one," she always says.

"Liam's f-f-fine." I'm shivering, even my voice. "But can't you hear her? The Banshee?"

"Shh! You'll wake your da. He has to be up at six."

"Listen." I'm listening myself . . . but now I hear nothing. She's gone.

I grab hold of my mother's nightdress and say, "She was here. I heard her."

My mother nudges me out into the hall. "Get back to your bed, love. You'll catch your death of cold. It was only a bad dream you were having, Terry. Or maybe you heard the owl in the oak tree. Or the Flannerys' cat. It skirls many a night."

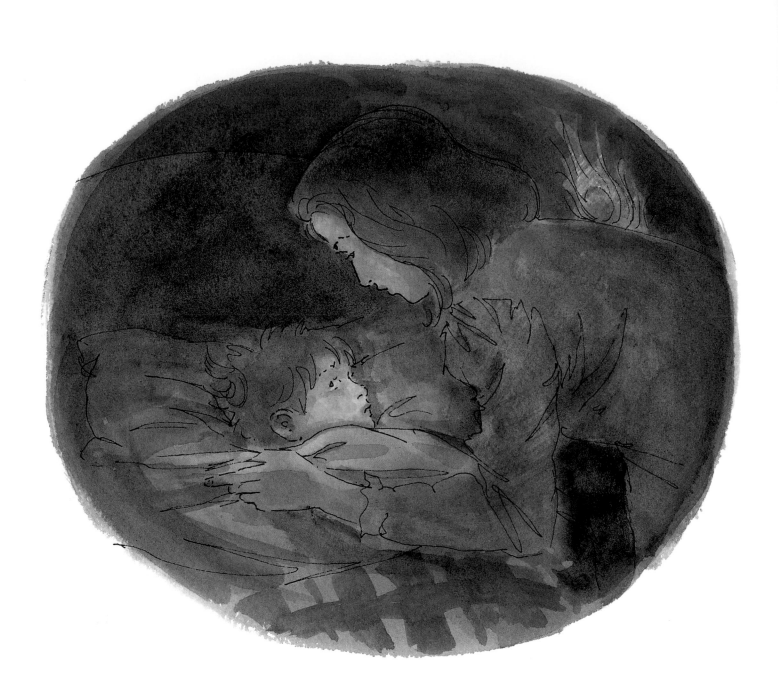

She holds my arm and hurries me into my bed. I pull the eiderdown up to my chin and listen hard. There's not a sound, not even the wind.

"Go to sleep now," my mother says. "And remember, the Banshee is just a superstition." She smiles, kisses the top of my head, and touches Liam's hunched shoulder.

"Leave the door open," I whisper.

I lie there, listening, but there's nothing to hear. I wish I could stop thinking about what Colin Maguire told me. He saw the Banshee once. He'd been coming home from a concert at the Hibernian Hall late one night when he heard her screeing outside McCaffery's house.

Old Mr. McCaffery was very sick. Colin said the Banshee was there, standing beside the hedge. She had on a long black robe, like a nun's, only hers was made of cobwebs. Her face was nothing but bones, and Colin said she looked right at him, and her eyes were two black stones.

Colin said he let out a squeal that would wake the dead. He turned himself around and began running, and the Banshee called something after him, but he couldn't understand what it was. He said her voice was a graveyard voice, pit gravel in it. He said he wet himself, but I was never to tell anybody that part. And a week later old Mr. McCaffery died.

Who is she after in our house? I wonder. My mum, my da, Liam . . . or me? Likely it's Liam, since he's the delicate one.

I wish Colin hadn't told me any of it. Then I wouldn't be thinking about the Banshee now. Anyway, he's always making up stories. My mother says: "That Colin Maguire has a great imagination!"

I'm almost asleep, my bad thoughts emptied out, when I hear it again.

"SCREE . . . SCREE . . ."

My heart starts battering inside me.

She's back.

I'm afraid to close my eyes.

In the shine of the moon I see my peacock feather on the table. My da bought it for me from a tinker. It's shimmering, bright blue, like spilled petrol, like Lough Corrib with the sun on it. It's my best thing.

I keep looking at it, and then I think, it could be an offering. For her.

I'd give it to her. Then I'd ask her to go away and leave our family be.

You'll never do it, Terry, I think. And then I think, *Yes, I will*.
I force myself out of bed, and I lift the feather from its jar.
My hand's shaking.

It's dark on the stairs. No windows to let the moonshine in.
Our big stove glows in the kitchen. The fire never goes out.
"It's the heart of the house," my mother always says.

I open the back door. The kitchen heat rushes out, and the night rushes in.

I can't go into that dark yard. Where *she* is. I can't. I go.

The grass is wet. I slither under the clothesline, where one of my da's shirts jumps in the wind, its sleeves like arms.

Shadows seep under the poplars. Their tops sway, dancing their own slow dance.

"SCREE . . . SCREE . . ."

Louder now. Louder out here. And then I see her.

She's crouched against the back wall, small and black,
wailing those awful wails.

I'm terrified.

I can't go closer.

I hold the peacock feather in front of my face and peer through it as it shifts and ripples.

I take a step . . . two. What if she calls out to me in her graveyard voice with the pit gravel in it?

I'm ready to run.

I lick my lips. "Banshee?" I whisper. "I've come to ask you to go away. I think you've come to the wrong house. Our Liam's very well. Thank you," I add.

She's not speaking. I try to see her, though I don't want to. The face of bones, the eyes that are two black stones.

I make myself move closer. "I've brought you a present. Here." I hold out the peacock feather. "It's my best thing."

The moon comes clear and bright as the wind sweeps the mizzle of cloud away from its face, and I stare.

There's no Banshee. There's only our big old tin bucket with the hole in the bottom. It's lying on its side, and there's something over it. I hunker down, move closer, tug on an edge of whatever is covering the bucket. It's one of my mother's black shawls, blown down from the clothesline. I drop it, then I pick up the bucket, and as I do, the wind makes a thinner wail through the hole.

"Scree . . . scree . . ."

I slump over myself. No Banshee. No dark ghost coming for one of us. I'm limp with relief.

I tip the bucket upside down and throw my mother's shawl back over the clothesline.

Everything in the yard is quivering—the trees, my da's shirt,
the clouds and moon in the sky above me. Shadows everywhere.
One moves, over by the hedge.

Suddenly, I'm scared again. Is she still there, watching me? Fast as I can, I stick the peacock feather through the hole in the bucket, just in case.

"This is for you!" I shout into the wind.
Then I run.

31

Back home to my own safe bed.